WHISPER TO THE SKY

KIM SIGAFUS

7th GENERATION
Summertown, Tennessee

Library of Congress Cataloging-in-Publication Data
available upon request.

7th Generation
Book Publishing Company
PO Box 99, Summertown, TN 38483
888-260-8458
bookpubco.com
nativevoicesbooks.com

ISBN: 978-1-939053-38-1

27 26 25 24 23 22   1 2 3 4 5 6 7 8 9

hildren aren't born bullies. Their world teaches them how to behave. Bullying is the result of deeply buried anger and frustration, combined with lost hope. This book is dedicated to all who are unable to express themselves. May we learn how to listen and hear what is said and what is unsaid. When we listen, we learn. When we learn, we become better people.

CONTENTS

An Urban Indian

S ydney sat in the front passenger seat of the car while her mother drove into the inner city of Minneapolis. The moving truck in front of them was being driven by a friend of her mother's and held everything they owned.

Sydney sighed and stared out the window, seeing nothing but big tall buildings and lot of traffic. It was nothing like home.

Her mother, Dakotah, had divorced Sydney's father, and now they were moving out of White Earth. Not wanting to deal with the talk around town, her father had moved off the reservation as well. In the blink of an eye, Sydney's life had changed forever.

The last conversation her parents had was a week before her father moved away.

"You think you can raise her better, Dakotah? Then go at it," he had yelled, slamming the door on his way out. Sydney had watched his car squeal out of the driveway and barrel down the street, until it was out of sight. She let the curtain fall and she started to cry.

That was the last time Sydney had shown any emotion. She had quietly packed the boxes her mother had given her and then helped put them in the moving truck. This morning, she grabbed her pillow with one hand and a blanket she'd had since she was a baby with the other. She opened the passenger-side door of their sedan and climbed in. With the pillow pushed up against the door, Sydney closed her eyes to block out her new reality. She didn't want to watch as they drove away from the only house she had ever known.

Sydney was on her way to becoming what she had always despised: an urban Indian. How do people keep the traditions of Native life when they are living in a big city? It just can't be done, she thought.

"We're almost there," her mother said, bringing Sydney's thoughts back to the present. She sat up and put her pillow in her lap.

Bam! A pothole caught them both off guard.

"Shoot," Dakotah said. "Don't they fix their roads here?"

Glancing out the window, Sydney saw a row of tired-looking houses on a block with few trees on it. It was now late afternoon, and there was no one outside. Her stomach growled, and she turned toward her mother.

"I'm hungry."

"I know, honey," Dakotah said, pulling the car next to the curb in front of a blue house. "But we only have so many hours to unload before we lose daylight. I'll see about ordering a pizza later."

Sydney sighed and opened the door to get out. She was stiff, and she yawned and stretched for a moment. Glancing around her, she watched her mother's friend Mary open up the back of the moving truck. She had helped them load it back at the reservation and then drove it to the new house for them. Now Mary surveyed the neatly stacked boxes.

"Do you have the keys, Dakotah?" Mary asked Sydney's mother.

"Yeah, they are supposed to be under a huge rock in the side lawn."

"Well, go get them while I secure the truck's door. We need to get rolling so I can head back home."

"You're going home tonight?" asked Sydney, clutching her pillow and blanket.

"That's the plan."

"You could stay with us until tomorrow. It will be easier to drive back in the daylight."

"I have to work in the morning, Sydney," replied Mary, as she pulled out boxes and set them on the ground. "So I need to leave as soon as we're done. I have to bring the truck back before I can head home and go to bed."

"Oh."

Mary paused to glance over at Sydney. She sighed and reached out for the girl.

"It's going to be okay," she said, kissing the top of Sydney's head.

Sydney shrugged and closed her eyes against the pain of having to watch Mary go, too. It seemed like everyone she loved was leaving. It was only her and her mother now, and that scared her to death.

"Look at that," Mary said, pointing to the blue house. "That's your new home. You get your own room, and your mother said there is a bathroom across the hall from it." She lifted the tip of Sydney's chin with her forefinger, and grinned. "I have never owned a house with two bathrooms in it."

"Mom didn't tell me about the bathroom situation," replied Sydney, taking a step back. "I guess that's kind of awesome."

"Come on in here," Dakota called out from the front door, waving to the two of them to come inside.

Mary and Sydney each grabbed a box and headed into the house. Sydney set her box down on the carpeted floor inside the entryway and surveyed the place. It was bigger than the house she had lived in on the reservation. This one had a large living room to the right, and a smaller room to the left.

"I wonder if this is an office," she muttered to herself. It very well could be, she thought, with its big windows on two sides and a real hardwood floor. And there were French doors that shut off the room from the rest of the house.

"That's going to be my office," said Dakotah, coming up behind her. "I plan to work at home for a while."

"Your new job is going to let you do that?" Sydney asked.

"At least for the first week. Then we'll see."

"That'll be different."

"Yes, it will." Dakotah looked at Sydney warmly and touched her daughter's arm. "I know this is all new to you, but I think you're going to fit in here just fine."

"How do you know?" Sydney asked doubtfully.

"Well, that's what I'm hoping." Her mother's smile dropped from her face and she squared her shoulders. "I have never bought a house on my own before. I've never raised a child on my own before, either. With your father missing-in-action, we're going to have to make a new life for ourselves." She shrugged and smiled. "All we have right now is each other."

With that, the conversation ended. Sydney took a tour of the house before she went back out to continue helping Mary unload the moving van. There were three bedrooms and an attached garage. She liked it, but it wasn't what she was used to. With her mom's new job, though, they were finally able to afford a place that was a little nicer.

Two hours later, it was dark, but the van had been unpacked and secured. Mary stood in the doorway of the blue house, talking with Dakota and Sydney.

"Are you sure you don't want to call off work for tomorrow?" asked Dakotah. "The drive will seem even longer if you're tired."

"I wish I could," replied Mary. "I certainly am tired, but I can't afford to take a day off. I don't have any vacation, you know."

Dakotah reached out to hug her best friend. "Okay then. Please let me know you got back alright. Call me if you get sleepy, and we can talk for a while."

"I will. Don't you worry about me, alright? I will be fine." Mary reached out to include Sydney in their hug. "And you . . . everything is going to be fine. Your mom is not going to sign you up for school until all your stuff is unpacked and you guys are settled in. That will give you at least a week to get used to things around here."

Mary pulled away and glanced from Sydney to Dakotah. "I sure will miss you guys. Visit whenever you want."

"If you get some time off, let us know. There's always a place for you here," said Dakotah. She sniffed, fighting back tears. Mary gave her another quick hug before stepping away and heading down the steps. She walked quickly to the truck, started it up, and then headed down the road. Dakotah closed the door and turned to look at Sydney.

"She doesn't like emotional goodbyes. She told me that before," said Dakotah, as she brushed away a tear. She took a deep breath and looked around. "Grab your phone and see which pizza places deliver. I have our address written on a piece of paper in my purse. Go get it and order us a large pizza with whatever you want on it. I'm going to go through the boxes and try to find the bedding."

"Are we putting up the beds tonight?" Sydney asked.

"Do you want to?"

Sydney thought about it and then glanced at her mother. She was smiling, but there was tiredness around her eyes. Sydney shook her head.

"No, let's just camp out for tonight," she decided. "We can have pizza and pop and then go to sleep. We can start fresh in the morning."

"Are you sure you want to sleep on the floor?" Dakotah asked.

"I'm fine with it," said Sydney. "Let's sleep here in the living room for tonight."

"Alright then."

The two went their separate ways for a while and met back in the living room. Sydney had ordered the pizza and pop, and Dakotah had made two makeshift beds next to each other on the floor. Sydney grabbed her pillow and blanket and set them on her temporary bed.

Dakotah glanced down. "I can't believe you still have that blanket," she mused, pointing to it. "How come you hang onto it?"

Sydney shrugged. "It's soft and comforting."

Dakotah caught her eyes and shook her head. "I'm so sorry all this has happened. I thought your dad and I would be together forever. It's just that . . . well, he changed. He used to be funny and he loved to goof around. Now he's so serious and restrained. He never hugged me anymore. We never . . . well, anyway, I still love him. I just can't live with him anymore. I deserve better."

Sydney smiled. "Good for you, Mom."

"What?"

"Good for you for thinking about yourself for once."

"Are you being sarcastic?"

Sydney shook her head. "No. I just want you to be happy. I know how difficult Dad is to live with. I lived with him, too, you know."

"He was always hard on you."

Sydney looked down at the floor. "I felt like I could never please him."

"I know. I saw it in your eyes whenever he would talk to you."

"Why did you let him speak to me that way?"

Dakotah took a deep breath, then slowly let it out. "I guess I thought a little bit of that would push you to do better, but he started taking it too far. I tried to talk to him, but he would always pull out the education card."

"What's that?"

"He has more education than I do. So, according to him, he knows more about child-rearing than I do."

"But, you're my mother!"

"True. But he is well educated and thinks he has better methods for dealing with you."

"*Dealing* with me? What I needed from him I never got."

"Sydney . . ."

"He never hugged me. He never told me how proud he was of me. He never said he loved me . . ."

Dakotah pulled her daughter into her arms as Sydney started to cry.

"We are better off without him," Sydney said, her voice muffled as she cried into her mother's shirt. "He is not fit to be anyone's father."

"Sydney, that's enough." Dakotah drew back and looked her daughter in the eye. "We are not going to talk about your dad behind his back."

"But . . ."

"It's not productive, and it's mean-spirited."

Sydney crossed her arms. "You're too forgiving."

"I haven't forgiven him yet," Dakotah replied. "But he is your father, and he did the best he could. That's all anyone can do."

"That's his *best*?" Sydney snorted.

"Do you remember Grandpa?" Dakotah asked.

"Of course I do, but what does that . . ."

"He was a tough old man. He was hard on your dad."

"So?"

"They say a man discovers how to be a dad by watching his own father. It's learned behavior," Dakota explained.

"I would think he would have figured out that how his father treated him was the wrong way to parent," Sydney said.

"It's easy to fall back on old habits or something you're used to." Her mother caught her eye and gave her the "mother" look. "Didn't I hear about some bullying that happened at the rez school that involved you and another student?"

"Well, I . . ."

"The apple doesn't fall far from the tree, I would say."

"Are you saying I'm like Dad?"

"I'm saying that maybe you learned how to do that from seeing how your father treats people. Most bullies are not happy with their lives, and bringing others down makes them feel better about themselves."

Sydney was quiet for a moment. Dakotah watched as her words began to sink in, and she wondered what Sydney was thinking.

"Mom, Autumn and I came to peace with each other before I left," Sydney said.

"Good to hear."

"I'm sorry I treated her that way."

"Does she know that?" Dakotah asked.

"I think so. We did talk about it a little."

"As long as she knows how sorry you are, that's what counts," Dakotah stated.

The doorbell rang, and they both jumped at the sound.

"That's an awful doorbell," said Sydney with a grin.

"It sounds like a sick donkey," replied her mother with a chuckle as she headed for the door.

They ate supper and shut off the overhead light. Sydney climbed under the covers, closed her eyes, and considered what her mom had said. She had thought she handled the Autumn situation well, but now she wasn't so sure. She had never actually told Autumn she was sorry. Maybe she should write her a letter or call her or something.

Yawning, Sydney snuggled under the covers and drifted off to sleep.

CHAPTER 2

Trying to Fit In

Sydney pushed her locker shut, then rotated the dial on the lock several times to mix up the numbers. She had no trouble getting into her locker for the first time, but she wanted to make sure everyone else did.

She straightened some wrinkles out of her shirt, which had been stored in a black garbage bag during the move. Most of her clothes were wrinkled at the moment, as her mother couldn't find the iron, and throwing them in the dryer for a few minutes hadn't worked very well.

She had selected her clothes carefully this morning, trying to decide what would make her look okay and fit in with the other students. She was well aware that jewel tones would complement her short black hair and Native skin, so she chose an emerald-green shirt with a pair of black pants. She wore her favorite high-top sneakers instead of her moccasins, hoping they would help her fit in better.

Her mother had commented on how dressy she looked.

"Change the shoes," her mother had advised, but Sydney had decided against that. She was going for the dressy-casual look.

She reached up to touch her shiny black hair, which she was still trying to get used to. Gone were the long locks down to her waist, and in their place was a short bob barely touching her shoulders. Her mother had cried when the beautician cut Sydney's hair, but Sydney had a new life, and she considered the haircut part of shedding her old one. In her culture, it was said that men cut their hair in anguish over the loss of someone, and that's how Sydney felt. No matter how indifferent her dad had been toward her, Sydney loved the father who had chosen to take himself out of her life. She would have to start over, and that included a new look.

Sighing, she turned around and started down the hall, glancing above each door to see the room numbers. She was looking for room 303, English class. When she spotted it, relief flashed in her eyes and she hurried toward it.

Seconds later, her books and pencil were flying across the floor. Not paying attention, she had bumped into someone who was now standing across from her, scowling. The girl's papers were scattered around them, and as Sydney glanced over at her, the girl crossed her arms as her eyes narrowed.

"Really? Are you blind?"

"Wh . . . what?" Sydney hesitated and then dropped down to the floor to gather her books. She had to chase after her pencil, which had rolled farther down the hall than she thought.

"So, you are blind *and* stupid. I see."

The girl bent down to retrieve her papers quickly and then straightened back up to give Sydney one more look before heading into room 303.

Sydney hesitated and then slowly followed the girl in.

The teacher looked up as she entered, and then gave the room a glance, pointing to a chair at a table in the front left of the room. There were two boys already sitting there, and Sydney was not excited to be the only girl at the table.

Some of the students watched as Sydney crossed the room; others just ignored her. Sydney slipped quickly into her chair and faced forward, knowing she was being observed. She could feel her cheeks getting hot and was grateful for her Native coloring, which she hoped helped hide the blush.

"Class, we have a new student," said the teacher, standing to face the group. "Hey!" he called out, pointing to the rear of the room. "You two in the back, that's enough!" The teacher sighed and then began again.

"Her name is Sydney, and she comes to us from White Earth."

"Did ya go to the rez school?" a boy in the back asked, then laughed. "You some kind of squaw or something?"

"Paxton, that's enough." The teacher threw a stern look at him, which only made the boy smirk.

"I'm sure if she wants you to know something about herself, she'll tell you," he added, sitting down at this desk. "Now, pull out a sheet of paper and start taking some notes."

Sydney could feel the other students looking at her with curiosity, but she caught no one's eye and did as she was told.

Fifty minutes later, she gathered her stuff together and waited for the bell to ring. She noticed the teacher had retreated to the back of the room to speak to the boys, who apparently hadn't turned in their homework. The bell rang, and Sydney stood up, grateful the class was over. Hopefully things would go better in the next one.

"Sydney is not a Native name."

Sydney froze and looked at the three girls who had surrounded her. One of them was the girl she had bumped into earlier.

"Ah . . . no," she said, pulling her books closer to her. "Excuse me," she added, trying to move past them.

They moved aside to let her through but followed her out the door.

"So, your whole family is not Native?" one of the girls asked.

Sydney didn't bother turning around to see who was speaking to her. As she walked, she pulled out the paper with her classes on it to see which room she needed to go to next. A moment later it was gone, as someone had plucked it out of her hands.

Stopping in the middle of the hall, Sydney reached for her paper, but it was pulled away from her.

"She has math with Mr. B. and then lunch," one of the girls said.

"And then she is in my history class," said the girl Sydney had run into earlier.

The third girl nodded, not saying much. She was staring at Sydney with a look of boredom.

"Come on, let's go," she said. "We're going to be late for class."

"Not if it looks like we are helping the new girl."

"If you want to help me, then tell me where my next class is," said Sydney, eying the girl she had run into earlier.

The girl shrugged. "I said it would *look* like we were helping you, not that we were actually going to do it."

Sydney grabbed her schedule back. "Then leave me alone, please."

She turned to go but could hear the girls laughing behind her.

"Nice shirt," yelled one of the girls. "Too bad you can't fill it out."

Sydney looked down at her too-skinny frame and started to walk quicker. Turning the corner, she ran into a teacher, who reached out to steady her.

"Hang on a minute," she said, frowning down at her. "Are you alright?"

Sydney nodded, not looking up. The teacher smiled and took a step back.

"Hello. I'm Ms. Howard. You appear to be lost. Are you new?"

Sydney nodded again, glancing at Ms. Howard, who reached for Sydney's class schedule.

"Okay, it seems that you are in Mr. Lehman's music class next. Do you play an instrument or sing?"

"I sing," Sydney replied, and Ms. Howard nodded.

"Good," said Ms. Howard. "I look forward to hearing you at the next concert. So, you will have to go back the way you came. Mr. Lehman's class is two doors down from the room you just left."

Sydney hesitated and then reached out to take the schedule back.

"Thank you," she said quietly and hesitantly started back down the hall. As she rounded the corner, she could see the girls still standing outside the English classroom door, talking and laughing. Sydney paused at the corner and glanced back at the teacher, who was frowning now. The teacher started down the hall toward Sydney and then stopped next to her.

"Is there a problem?" Ms. Howard asked, glancing down the hall. When she spied the three girls, she nodded.

"I see you've met Amelia, Maci, and Riley."

When Sydney turned questioning eyes to the teacher, the teacher pointed down the hall.

"The three girls standing outside the door down there," Ms. Howard said.

Sydney nodded. "I didn't know their names, but they were in my English class."

"I see." Ms. Howard studied Sydney. "Have they been giving you trouble?"

"Um, not really," Sydney answered. She could see the girls stare at them and then begin moving down the hall toward them.

"Hi, Sydney," said Riley with a grin. "Nice shirt."

The teacher's eyes narrowed at Sydney's downcast expression. She glanced at the girls and saw them grinning at Sydney.

"You girls have thirty seconds to get to class or you'll be tardy," she said.

"Well, we did spend some time trying to help Sydney find her next class," replied Amelia with a pointed look at Sydney. Sydney shook her head to speak but the teacher cut her off.

"So, you're the ones responsible for sending her the wrong way to a classroom that was just down the hall from her last one?"

"Well, I . . ." Amelia stopped and glanced at Sydney again, but Sydney remained silent.

"Well, I told her where it was. I can't help it if she can't follow directions," answered Amelia with plenty of attitude, shifting her books to her other hand. "Let's go girls. We'll be late for class."

"Just a minute, Amelia," Ms. Howard said. "I don't appreciate the way you're talking to me. I think the principal would like to hear about this. And I'm not sure you didn't misdirect Sydney on purpose. This is not the way we welcome new students to our school. Please follow me."

Ms. Howard started walking down the hall, and the girls reluctantly followed, glaring at Sydney as they passed by her. Sydney sighed and turned to go down the hall to her classroom, slipping inside just as the bell rang. The teacher looked up and smiled as Sydney took a seat in the back of the classroom this time.

As the teacher started to speak, Sydney's thoughts turned to her encounter with the girls and Ms. Howard. She realized Ms. Howard was only trying to help, but she also was aware that it would make things worse for her in the long run. That's because Sydney had been just like Amelia at her last school. She knew the girls would never let this go. They were going to blame her for getting into trouble.

Sydney tried her best to concentrate on what the teacher was saying. But she couldn't wait for this day to end.

Could It Get Any Worse?

Several days passed, and Sydney was depressed. She lived close enough to walk to and from school, and today she had been harassed again by some girls who "accidently" bumped into her as she walked home. She had slipped and landed in mud. The echoes of laughter followed her down the block as she quickly got up, picked up her book bag, and slowly started walking again.

She hated school. She absolutely, without a shadow of a doubt, hated everyone there, too. Most of them were standoffish, and no one talked to her. She missed the rez school, where all her friends were.

Sydney sighed as she entered her house and walked down the hall to her room. She pulled off her muddy clothes, throwing them in the green hamper by the door. Then she slipped on a pair of sweatpants and a T-shirt and went into the kitchen to have a snack.

Eating an apple, Sydney wandered into the living room and sat on the couch. She wondered what her friends from the rez were doing right now. Were they over at Bre's doing homework, or at Jayden's house on the trampoline? She sighed, taking another bite of apple.

Well, it's not like she hadn't accomplished anything here, she mused. In the past couple of days, she had managed to make enemies with the most popular girls in school. That meant no one wanted to go near her for fear they would be harassed, too.

The boys just stared at her, and the girls did their best to ignore her. The few times she tried to reach out to someone, she had been met with silence or they had turned and walked away. She didn't understand what was going on. Surely those girls couldn't have told everyone to ignore her. Surely someone there would be interested in getting to know her. Sitting alone at lunch every day was not her idea of a good time.

She didn't know how to fit in. Her clothes were similar to those worn by others. She kept her hair simple; she didn't do anything fancy with it. She made sure she wore nothing "Native" that would make her stand out in that respect. Was she going to go through the whole school year with no friends?

"I want to go home," she muttered, setting her apple core on the coffee table in front of her. "I hate this place."

Just then, the door flew open, as her mother pushed her way in with several bags of groceries in her hands. Sydney rushed over to help her, and together they managed to get everything in the kitchen. After she set her bags on the counter, Sydney started digging into them, looking for chips, or candy, or something good to eat.

"Stay out of the bags unless you're going to put the groceries away," instructed her mother. "I'm going to start supper in a few minutes."

Sydney did as she was told and started to help her mother. A few minutes later, she plopped down in one of the kitchen chairs.

Her mother glanced over at her as she started to brown the hamburger.

"Everything alright? How was school today?"

"Fine."

"Have you made any friends?"

"No."

"No?"

"No."

"I'm sorry to hear that."

"Mom, will we ever be able to go back to the rez again? I miss my friends."

"I know you do, Sydney, but we bought this house. It's ours. I don't want to go back there with everyone talking about us and your father." Her mother shook her head resolutely. "No, I'm not going back there. I'm going to make a new life for us here."

Sydney went quiet and then got up from her chair. "I have homework," she muttered as she got up. "Call me when supper's done."

Dakotah watched her daughter leave the room. It was obvious that Sydney was unhappy living here. She hadn't made any friends and was lonely. Starting over was hard, and even she was a little lonely.

She stirred the hamburger and then added seasonings to it as she thought about her new job. The people there had been very welcoming and let her settle in first before expecting a lot of work out of her. She'd done office work before and was a fast typist, which had gotten her the job in the first place. She was also trained on the many computer applications the business used. She would be a good employee for them.

As Dakotah was straining the grease out of the hamburger, her cell phone rang. She quickly put down the pan to answer it.

"Hello?"

"It's Roger."

Dakotah's heart skipped a beat, and she sat down at the little table in the kitchen.

"Yes?"

"I would like to see my daughter."

"That's new."

"Now don't start . . ."

"Look, she doesn't want to see you. The judge said he would leave it up to her since she's old enough to make that decision herself."

"Let me talk to her."

"She is doing her homework right now."

"She can't sacrifice a few moments of her time to talk to her father? I have a right to see her."

"Like I said, that's up to her . . ."

"No, it's not! We're her parents!" Roger shouted. "I want to see her. I can just imagine what poisonous things you've said about me. No wonder she . . ."

"I have said nothing about you," said Dakotah, her voice a little louder now. "I don't have to. She lived with you, too. She knows what you're like."

"You little . . ."

"Mom, let me speak to him."

Dakotah turned to see Sydney standing behind her.

"Honey, you don't have to do this," Dakotah began, but she was interrupted by Roger.

"Put her on the phone . . . now!"

Sydney reached out her hand, and Dakotah reluctantly handed her the phone.

"Dad?"

"Sydney, I want to see you."

"What did you have in mind?"

"I want your mother to drive you over to see me next weekend."

"Where do you live?"

"Didn't your mother tell you? I moved to Onamia."

"Dad, that's got to be a couple of hours away . . ."

"It's an hour and a half."

"How long would I stay?"

"Friday to Sunday."

"Then you'd drive me home Sunday?"

"No, your mother can come back and get you."

"That's not fair," replied Sydney. "You should drive one way at least."

"Not fair? Your mother took you away from me. She should have to pay for that."

"*You* drove us away from you, Dad."

"Don't speak to me like that, young lady."

"No, Dad, I will not be coming next weekend. I will not put Mom out like that. If you aren't willing to drive one way, then forget it."

"Now listen here . . ."

Sydney gave the phone back to her mother and turned around and left the room. Dakotah sighed and got back on the phone.

"She's gone," she said. "She doesn't want to see you."

"You did this. You told her she couldn't go. I'll drag you back into court if I have to, but I'm going to see my daughter."

"Okay then, drag me back into court. But in the meantime, stop calling and harassing me or I'll have my number changed. If Sydney wants to see you, she'll call you."

Dakotah slammed down the phone and sat shaking in the chair. If he dragged her back into court, she could lose Sydney.

After a moment, she got up and finished dinner. They ate in silence, each of them thinking about the phone call. Then Sydney did the dishes while her mother worked on the laundry. When she was done, Sydney headed for her bedroom.

At nine o'clock, Sydney came back out into the living room to say goodnight to her mother. She found her sitting on the couch with her legs tucked under her, drinking a cup of tea.

"I'm going to bed now," she said, and her mother nodded.

"Goodnight."

Sydney paused in the doorway and waited for her mother to say something more, but there was just silence. Sydney turned around and went back into her bedroom and prepared for bed.

Lying in bed with the covers tucked tightly around her, she stared at what she could see of the ceiling as thoughts of the phone conversation with her father ran through her head. A moment later, she could hear her mother softly crying in the living room. Sydney sat up in her bed and started to get up but thought better of it. She could go out there, but she didn't know what to say. She crawled back into bed and closed her eyes. A moment later, tears filled her eyes and spilled down her cheeks. She rolled over to put the pillow over her ears to try to block out the world.

When Dakotah checked on her an hour later, she found Sydney sprawled out on the bed, her cheeks stained with tears. She gently pulled the covers over her daughter and stepped back to watch her sleep. With a catch in her throat, her mother gave her one last look and then closed the door and walked away.

CHAPTER 4

I Want to Go Home!

S ydney was sitting in class doodling on her notebook when someone walked in and interrupted the teacher's lecture. She looked up and noticed they were both staring at her, and she frowned, wondering what was going on.

The teacher gestured, and Sydney got up and walked to the head of the room. Of course everyone was watching her, but she ignored them.

"Sydney, your father's here to see you," said her teacher quietly. "He would like to take you out of school for the day."

Sydney shook her head. "No."

"We know your parents are divorced, and we have a call in to your mother," said the office runner who delivered the message. "We're waiting for her to call back."

"I wish you hadn't done that," replied Sydney. "I am not going with him."

"Are you sure?"

"He isn't supposed to have me unless I decide, and definitely not without my mom knowing ahead of time."

"I see," replied the teacher. "There's a court order, then?"

"Yes." Without another word, Sydney walked back to her seat and sat down.

There was murmuring throughout the room. Sydney's teacher whispered something to the office runner and they left.

A few minutes later, there was a commotion down the hall. Her teacher poked his head out of the room, assessed the situation, and then quickly shut the door.

"Sydney, you and Bryson change places right now."

Both students looked at him in surprise and then jumped when the teacher raised his voice and repeated his request.

They both gathered their things and had just sat back down again when they heard a commotion outside the classroom door. Sydney had taken her seat in the back right corner of the room when she heard raised voices in the hall.

"I'm sorry, Mr. Coffman," said the principal. "You can't just go barging into every classroom like this. If you don't leave, the police will escort you off the premises."

"I have a right to see my daughter! That mother of hers has poisoned her against me."

"Maybe, but you don't have a right to bring your personal business into my school," replied the principal.

The doorknob jiggled, and as Sydney held her breath, there was a loud bang, as someone apparently pushed the door closed again.

"She's not in there," said the principal calmly.

While almost everyone in class was staring at the door, Sydney remembered that there was a little window in it. She wondered if her father was looking through that window trying to find her.

She glanced at the teacher, who shushed the class as the door opened a crack.

"Mr. James, is Sydney in here?" asked the principal.

"Nope."

"Thank you."

The door closed, and for a few moments, no one spoke. Sydney realized that she was moved because she had been sitting in the line of sight of the little window. In moving her, the teacher had protected her from possibly having to face an uncomfortable situation with her father.

She started to shake. The whole scene had unnerved her, and for the first time in her life, she was afraid of her father.

After school, Sydney headed out the side door of the building and started walking down the block. She was trying to think of any way to get home without having to walk her usual route, since the bullies couldn't seem to leave her alone.

"Sydney?"

She stopped short when she saw her mother's car pull up alongside of her.

"Get in," her mother said, and Sydney did as she was told.

"I was watching for you," said her mother, glancing at her. "I saw you slip out the side door. Why did you do that? Don't you normally go out the front like everyone else?"

Talking about her bullying situation was not something Sydney wanted to get into at the moment, so she remained silent.

"The school called me about your dad."

Sydney nodded but kept staring straight ahead.

"I'm sorry he did that to you," said her mother, taking a left turn down the road to their house. "He had no right to embarrass you like that."

Sydney gritted her teeth but still remained silent.

"Are you alright?"

"I'm fine."

"You don't sound fine."

"Well, I'm as fine as I'm going to get at the moment. Dad barged into the school making a commotion outside my classroom. The police had to be called to remove him, and the kids already think I'm a freak, so this just made it worse." Sydney turned to look at her mom. "I want to go home."

"We *are* going home."

"No! I want to go back to the reservation school. *That's* my home . . . where my friends are. No one likes me here, and I think they're all pretty stupid."

"Sydney . . ."

"I don't fit in here, Mom," she said. "I've tried. I wear the same type of clothing they do, I don't wear braids or look Native . . ."

"Sounds like you are losing your identity, Sydney. You should be yourself."

"I'm *trying* to lose myself! I don't want to be different from everyone else." Sydney shook her head. "You don't understand, Mom. They don't like me *because* I am Native. They call me 'squaw,' among other things."

"You can't be the only Native in the whole school."

"I'm not, and they don't give me a hard time. They just ignore me." Sydney went silent for a moment and then added, "There's a difference between an urban Native kid and a rez Native kid, Mom."

Dakotah frowned. "Which is?"

"At the rez school, you can just be yourself. Everyone understands the culture." Sydney shook her head. "Here, they don't like that I am different, and they sure don't want to take the time to understand the culture."

"We haven't been here very long," her mother pointed out. "Maybe in time . . ."

"In time?" Sydney laughed bitterly. "No one likes me now; they're sure not going to like me later."

"Don't you think you're exaggerating a little bit?"

Sydney turned to stare at her mother. "No one talks to me. When they do, it's to make fun of my clothes, my skin, the way I dress, whatever they don't like."

"What? How long has this . . .?"

"And, it takes me so long to walk home because they're harassing me all the way there!"

Her mother glanced over at her. "Sydney, why didn't you tell me this before? I'll call the school and put a stop to that immediately."

"No, Mom. That will only make it worse."

"I don't think . . ."

"Yes, it will! I didn't want to tell you in the first place because I knew you would do something like that."

Her mother shook her head. "Well, you can't just expect me to sit by and let people harass you."

Sydney sighed. "Look, there's nothing you can do."

"Of course there is," her mother answered, getting upset now. "The principal could get involved, for one thing."

"I don't want any more attention than I'm already getting, Mom. I'm just trying to blend in. Please don't do anything."

"Well, what are you going to do then?"

"Nothing for now."

"That doesn't seem like a good plan."

"I don't have a plan, Mom. I have very little control over my life right now."

Her mother pulled into the alley and drove up to the garage. Sydney pushed the button on the garage door and they drove inside. Her mother shut off the car and turned to look at Sydney.

"I will let this go for now, but I want you checking in with me every couple of days about it. Do you understand? If the situation doesn't get better soon, I want to know. You are still my daughter, and I have a right to know what's going on."

"And Dad?"

"Let me handle your dad."

"What are you going to do?"

"I'm going to go back to court and have his visitation rights changed. He's lost his mind, and I don't want you around that."

"He's acting the way he always has," Sydney pointed out.

"Yes, and that's unacceptable. I won't deal with it anymore."

"What will you ask for in court?"

"Supervised visitation might work. I don't trust him. And, frankly, I think the school would be happy to provide the court with an account of his behavior today."

"He's just frustrated he can't see me."

"First of all, don't defend him. What he did was out of line. Second of all, you don't want to see him. You told him that on the phone."

"I told him he had to agree to drive halfway and meet us or drive one way, at least."

"Which he didn't agree to." Dakotah shook her head. "We are no longer married, and he has gone above and beyond what he's allowed to do. No, this behavior is going to stop or he will no longer get the chance to see you."

"But, Mom . . ."

"No, this is my decision. When you are eighteen, you can decide for yourself. In the meantime, what I say goes. I may have agreed not to have a say right now over the bullying issues you're going through, but I have a say in this."

With that, Dakotah opened the door and got out, slamming it behind her.

Sydney sighed and opened her car door. After shutting it quietly, she trailed behind her.

Knowing her mother, she knew that was the end of the conversation for now. But she realized her mother was not going to allow her daughter to be harassed. She just hoped she could come up with a way to handle the situation before her mother got involved.

CHAPTER 5

A Kindred Soul

Sydney took her lunch tray and walked to the back of the cafeteria. She sat down at a long table and slid down to the end nearest the wall.

After opening her milk, she looked out over the lunchroom and sighed, leaning back against the wall. She took a drink of cold milk and then set it back on the tray again next to a piece of pizza and an apple.

She always sat in the same spot, away from everyone else, where she could easily see all aspects of the room. She felt like a Wild West gunslinger sitting with her back against the wall so no one could sneak up on her.

In truth, she liked watching people. They were interesting creatures collectively, but kind of stupid taken one by one. All the girls seemed to talk about were the boys, and all the boys seemed to talk about were the girls . . . and saving up for a car.

From her vantage point, she could also see into the kitchen. She liked watching the staff busily coming in and out, filling up trays with food, and talking with the students. No one paid her any attention, and she liked it that way.

A commotion caught her attention, and she glanced to the left to see some boys, pushing and shoving each other. A couple of them were laughing, and for a moment, she thought they were just goofing around. She started to turn away when she saw another boy rise off the floor and dust himself off.

He had short brown hair and was average height. There was nothing special about him, nothing that made him stand out, but he seemed to upset the others, because they kept pushing him around.

A teacher walked over and pointed to a table, and the boys reluctantly left the guy they were messing around with alone. Sydney watched as the teacher talked for a moment with the brown-haired boy, and then she watched him slowly get up and walk away. She frowned, wondering what was going on, and then sat back down, realizing she had stood up to get a better look. She sighed, reached for the piece of pizza, and took a big bite.

"Can I sit here?"

Sydney's eyes flew up as she saw that the boy she had been watching was now standing next to her. She had a mouthful of food but nodded, chewing quickly and swallowing hard. She took a drink of milk to push the food all the way down and then stared at him as he dropped onto the bench across from her.

"Um . . . sure," she said, a little late since he was already sitting down.

The boy took a bite out of his apple and then glanced at her.

"You're Sydney, right? From the reservation school?"

Sydney gave him a nod and then looked down at her tray.

"I'm Finn," he said, and she nodded.

"Like Huck Finn?" she asked, and he laughed.

"No. Like Finnegan. My parents are from Finland." He shrugged. "I guess they miss their homeland, so they named me after it."

"I see."

"It also means 'brown,' and since I have brown hair, maybe that's why they named me that." He took another bite of apple. "I never asked them."

He eyed her a moment, and she flushed, looking away.

"What about you?" he asked. "'Sydney' isn't a Native name."

She shrugged. "Mom liked the name, I guess. Dad wanted me to have a Native name, but she won out." Sydney looked away. "It was one of the only arguments she ever won . . ." she muttered, trailing off.

"Yeah, I have parents like that, too," he said, setting his apple down for his piece of pizza. "They finally split up on account of me."

"You?"

He nodded, taking a bite of pizza. He chewed slowly and then sighed. "I came out last summer."

He went on to finish the pizza while Sydney stared at him.

"Came out?"

"Yeah, you know, I'm gay. I guess I've always known," he said, wiping his mouth with a napkin. "I mean, I wanted to be a fairy princess for Halloween."

"When?"

"When I was little. You know, five or six years old. My mom was really upset, but Dad just shrugged and said I could do what I want."

He took another bite of his apple. "Mom wouldn't take me trick-or-treating that year; Dad had to do it. From then on, they argued over everything—what I wore, what toys I could play with—you get the drill. Anyway, my mom finally had enough and left."

"I'm sorry."

He nodded. "Yeah, me too. I miss her. I came home from school one day and she was gone." He set his apple core down. "What about you? Are your parents together?"

Sydney shook her head. "They divorced and we moved here."

"Well, you sure are popular."

"What? Me?"

"Yeah. Everybody talks about you. They must like you."

Sydney sighed. "That's not why they talk about me. They all think I'm weird or something because I'm Native."

"Are you?"

"Am I what? Native? Yes, I am."

"No, I mean are you weird?"

Sydney sighed. "Probably."

"Good."

"Good?"

"Yeah. I mean, who would wanna be like everyone else? That's boring."

"I guess."

"Take my word for it. It's good to be different." He smiled. "I like that you're Native."

"Why?"

He shrugged. "It's an interesting culture. Will you teach me some things about it?"

"Maybe. Can I ask you something?"

"Sure."

"What was happening over by the lunch line earlier?"

"Oh, that. It's no big deal."

"It looked like a big deal."

He shrugged. "They know I'm gay, and they don't like it."

"How did they find out? Did you tell them?"

He shook his head. "I came out to my parents, not anyone else."

"Except me."

He smiled. "Yeah, I did come out to you, didn't I. But you didn't know me before. They did. It seems like the older I got, the more suspicious they got." He shrugged. "I couldn't hide it if I tried."

"I didn't notice."

"Were you looking?"

"Well, no."

He shrugged again. "That's why." He smiled at her, and she flushed again, looking away.

"So, since you're not as popular as I thought, maybe you could use a friend. How about if we stick together?"

"I . . ."

"Unless you have a problem with me being gay?"

"No."

He nodded. "Well, good. And I don't have a problem with you being Native."

Sydney smiled.

Finn leaned forward and pushed his tray away. "So, how am I doing so far?"

"What do you mean?"

"I mean, have I scared you away? Dad says I talk too much. Do I talk too much?"

"Yes."

"Yes?"

"Yes." She laughed at the look he gave her. "But it's okay," she added with a grin.

"Good." He sat back and glanced around a moment. Then he leaned forward and caught her eye.

"Wanna give them something new to talk about?" he asked with a twinkle in his eye.

"What do you mean?"

He reached out for her hand and she frowned, staring at him. A moment later, she put her hand in his. He grinned and glanced around again.

"They're looking at us," he whispered, and she looked around to see that he was right. She tried to pull away, but he held tight to her hand.

"Hang on a minute. Let's give them time to wonder what we are doing," he whispered again, and she shook her head. He gave her a wicked grin, and she couldn't help but smile back.

"You really like to push their buttons, don't you," she said as he slowly released her hand.

"It's what gets me through the day. So, do you bus or walk?"

"Walk."

"I used to do that, but I was getting harassed so much my dad had to start picking me up."

"I'm sorry to hear that."

"Do you want a ride home? If you walk, you must live close by."

"No . . . no, that's okay . . . I can . . ."

"I know you can walk," he said with a grin. "I've seen you do it."

"What?"

"Walk. You know, put one foot in front of the other."

She shook her head. "You need better jokes."

"You can tell me some on the way home."

"I don't think . . ."

"Good. Don't think. No worries. My dad is cool. Just meet me outside the front door right after school. My last class is by my locker. I will be there about five minutes after the bell."

He got up and grabbed his tray. "Are you done?"

She nodded as he grabbed hers, too.

"See you after school," he said, and he left.

Sydney got up and trailed behind him, heading back to class. She was fully aware that people were eyeing her as she walked past, probably wondering what she was doing with Finn.

As she grabbed the books from her locker, she went over the conversation she'd had with him. He had stepped into her life like a whirlwind of energy. She smiled. She liked him.

She shut her locker door and caught a glimpse of him down the hall. He waved as someone bumped into him on purpose. They laughed as he bent down to get his books. He straightened up, and for a moment, she caught a look of pain and embarrassment in his eyes before he turned away to walk down the hall.

A kindred soul.

An unfamiliar feeling of sympathy came over her, and she hesitated. Then, without giving it any more thought, she ran to catch up with him.

"Finn!"

He was just turning the corner when she caught up with him. She reached for his hand and then held it tightly as he turned to look at her in surprise.

"Wanna walk me to class?" she asked with a smile, and an emotion she couldn't quite catch flitted into his eyes and then out again. He smiled.

"Sure."

The voices in the hall went silent as Sydney and Finn turned the corner and disappeared.

Unexpected News

Her mother was in the kitchen when Sydney got home. She was just closing the dishwasher as Sydney walked into the house.

"Hey!" Dakotah called out. "You're home earlier."

"I got a ride."

Dakotah poked her head out of the kitchen as Sydney removed her shoes by the front door.

"A ride? From who?"

"My friend Finn."

"Finn?"

"Yup."

"You've never mentioned him before."

"I just met him."

"And you let him give you a ride home? I don't think . . ."

"It's okay, Mom. His dad drove me home."

"His dad?" Dakotah frowned as Sydney entered the kitchen and sat down at the breakfast nook.

Sydney caught her mother's look as she reached for a cookie.

"It's okay, Mom. They're nice people."

"I see. Well, I'm not sure I like people I don't know driving my daughter home."

"I was safe, Mom."

"But what do we know about them?"

"I know enough."

"Well, I don't."

"I need the ride home, Mom."

"It's not that far . . ."

"It's too far when people are messing with you all the way," countered Sydney.

"But . . ."

"Mom! You have to trust me. Everything is fine. Finn is great, and his father is nice."

Dakotah walked over to the sink and started to wash it out. "So, this Finn. Are you interested in him?"

Sydney started to laugh and then choked on part of her cookie. After a coughing fit and a drink of the water her mother had shoved at her, Sydney shook her head.

"He's just my friend."

"Are you sure, because maybe it's time we talk about certain things . . ."

"Oh, Mom, no. I don't need the talk. I know where babies come from."

"Good to hear, but you haven't started dating and . . ."

"I'm not dating! Mom, just relax. Finn is my friend."

"Are you sure? Because . . ."

"Mom, Finn's gay."

Dakotah's eyes flew open, and she stared at her daughter a moment.

"I see," she said, and Sydney glanced at her.

"You don't have anything against that, do you?"

Dakotah shook her head. "No, but I . . . no, I don't."

"Good. I have homework, so I'm going to start that. Let me know when supper's ready."

Dakotah watched her daughter leave the room. She could tell from the lightness of Sydney's step that she was finally finding some happiness in this new life. She didn't want to jinx that for her, but she was solely responsible for keeping her daughter safe, and she took that very seriously. She wondered about this Finn person and what he actually wanted from Sydney.

Her phone rang, and she wiped her hands on a kitchen towel and picked it up.

"Hello? Yes, this is her. Oh, hi, Marah." Dakotah sat down at the breakfast nook and settled in.

"I'm fine. Yes, Sydney is fine."

As she listened, the color drained from her face.

"What? What happened? How . . . I see. But I just saw her. She helped me move."

Dakotah's voice dialed down to a whisper. "When is it? Okay. Of course we'll be there. Bye."

Dakotah pulled the phone away from her face as the line went dead on the other end. She sat for a long time, not moving, wondering if this was somehow all a bad dream.

Sydney came in a while later to find her mother sitting in the same spot. The phone was sitting in front of her on the counter and her mother was silent.

"Mom? What are you doing?"

Dakotah turned her gaze to her daughter, and Sydney could see that she had been crying.

"Mom? What is it? What happened?" Sydney paused a moment and added, "Is it Dad?"

Dakotah shook her head and gathered herself together.

"No, it's Mary." Dakotah took a long, ragged breath. "She went to bed last night and never woke up."

"What? No . . ."

Sydney started to cry as she walked into the living room. Her mother trailed after her.

"Not Mary," whispered Sydney.

"I'm sorry, Sydney."

"She was your best friend."

"And yours."

The two sat down on the couch and held hands. Dakotah reached over for the tissue box and handed it to Sydney, who pulled a wad of it out to blow her nose.

"I've known her since grade school," said Dakotah. "I fell off the swing and she helped me back up."

"I've known her all my life," whispered Sydney.

"I know. She was there when you were born." Dakotah teared up again. "I don't know how I'm going to get through this life without her."

"I'm so sorry, Mom."

Dakotah dropped her head on Sydney's shoulder and sighed. "I'm all alone in this world now."

"No, you're not." Sydney pulled away to look at her mother. "You have me."

Dakotah nodded. "But parents are supposed to take care of their children, not the other way around."

"I'm not a child, Mother. We can take care of each other."

"I guess we'll have to now."

"We have been all along, you know."

"I guess so."

"Is there going to be a funeral?"

"Yes. Saturday afternoon."

"Are they going traditional?"

Dakotah nodded. "With some Christian burial rites added. She's going to be cremated, though. They are going to spread her ashes in Strawberry Lake near her parents' home."

"Can we go?"

"Of course. We will drive up after work and school on Friday."

"Where will we stay?"

"A hotel."

Sydney nodded, then sighed. "Will we only be there for the weekend?" she asked.

"Yes. We'll drive back Sunday. Do you want to call your friends to see if they want to get together while you are there? I know you said you're missing them."

"Yeah, maybe I will do that."

"Okay, good. Well, I'm going to make supper."

Dakotah got up and headed for the kitchen. Sydney pulled her phone out of her pocket and sent a message to her friends Jayden and Bre. They both answered back and agreed to meet on Saturday night to grab a bite to eat.

She shoved her phone back into her pocket and sat back on the couch, her legs curled up under her. It would be nice to see her friends again and catch up.

Her thoughts wandered to Finn, and she wondered what her friends would think of him. They probably wouldn't like the fact that he was gay and would wonder what she was doing making friends with someone like him. She knew if she had been back in the reservation school, she would have been part of the group of people who made fun of him. There was no way she would have ever been seen with him, that's for sure.

Sydney frowned as she thought about that. She wondered why things were different here. Why was her attitude about him different? She hadn't changed, had she? She liked Finn. But she had gotten to know him a little, and that would have never happened back on the rez. And she would have never felt sorry for him being harassed like that. She probably would have laughed at him.

"Sydney? Can you set the table? We'll be eating soon. I made soup and sandwiches."

Sydney pushed the thoughts away and got up to help her mom. A moment later, they were engrossed in deciding on a hotel, and all thoughts of Finn melted away.

What Goes Around, Comes Around

T he next day, Sydney looked for Finn in the school cafeteria and found him at a table alone. He looked depressed, and she wondered what had happened to put him in that mood.

She started for him, then paused. After all, she didn't know him that well, and maybe he wanted to be alone.

She watched him play with his milk carton for a moment and then decided she would put herself out there and see if he wanted company. After all, the worst he could say was no, right?

After taking a deep breath, she walked over and stood in front of him holding a tray full of food. He glanced up and warmth filled his eyes when he saw her.

"Hi," he said with a smile, and gestured to the spot across from him. She returned the smile and sat down.

"What's up?" she asked, opening her milk.

"What do you mean?"

"You look like your dog died." Sydney took a drink of milk as Finn smiled.

Shrugging, he replied, "I don't have a dog. But I have a mother, and she wants to see me."

"Is that bad?"

"Dad said he thought she was going to try to talk me out of my choices."

"Choices?"

"My gay choices."

"Oh. Is that a choice?"

"Not in my book, it isn't. But others have different views. Some think you can talk someone out of being gay." He sighed. "Like my mother."

"What's her problem with it? You know, in my culture, traditionally we hold people with alternate life choices in high esteem."

"You do?"

"Yes. They have chosen a difficult life path, and we give them a lot of credit for that."

"I wish I was Native."

Sydney smiled. "Or maybe that your mother was?"

"Yeah."

Sydney sighed. "Look, you are a reasonably intelligent guy."

"How do you know that? We just met yesterday."

"Because you've chosen to become my friend."

He laughed. "Oh, I see."

"That being said, listen to what she has to say. Everyone's entitled to their opinion. Think about it, and then respond."

"But I already know what she's going to say. She is going to tell me it's against God and . . ."

"Do you think so?"

Finn sighed and looked away. "I don't know," he muttered. "I'm not really into religion." He turned back to catch her eyes. "Do you believe in God?"

"I believe in *Gitchie Manitou*."

"What is that?"

"It's a who."

"Okay, *who* is that?"

"The Great Spirit."

"Isn't that the same thing?"

"Possibly. But . . ."

"So what are you two up to?"

Sydney and Finn glanced up to see Amelia standing in front of them.

"I can't possibly see what business it is of yours," answered Finn, staring at her.

Amelia glanced over at Sydney. "Two peas in a pod, huh? That's interesting news."

"Which I'm sure you would love to spread all over school," replied Finn, his eyes narrowing. "Sydney and I are friends and that's all. She doesn't need to deal with all your backstabbing lies as you amp up the rumor mill around here." He looked over at Sydney and then back up at Amelia. "Leave her alone."

Amelia shrugged, hugging her books closer to her chest. "Why should I? What are you going to do about it?"

Finn sat forward and pinned her with his eyes. "I'm sure your boyfriend would love to hear about your meetings behind the building with Paxton." His smile was not pleasant. "Isn't the dance coming up in a few weeks? I would hate for you to have to go alone."

"You . . ."

Finn shook his head. "Leave, Amelia. Now!"

Amelia started to say something and then closed her mouth and stomped away. Sydney held her breath until the girl was out of sight and then she turned back to Finn.

"I hope that didn't make things worse for me," she said.

Finn shook his head. "You just have to know how to deal with these people."

"I guess."

"And I have lots of practice."

"I'm sorry to hear that."

Finn shrugged. "I can handle it." He started to eat his almost-cold food, and Sydney followed suit. For a moment, no one spoke.

Finn finished off his milk, then asked, "Need a ride home today?"

She shook her head.

He glanced over at her and his eyes narrowed. "Hey, is everything alright?"

Sydney sighed. "I guess. I'm just worried about Amelia. They've been harassing me for weeks now."

"I know."

"You do?"

Finn nodded. "I saw you walking home from school a while back. I saw them bothering you." He paused, then added, "I thought perhaps I'd found a kindred soul."

Sydney smiled at his use of the words she had used to describe him earlier.

"But you said you thought I was popular," she replied.

"Initially, I did think that. I thought you were just goofing around with them. But then I started to listen to what was being said about you and realized I was wrong."

"What's being said about me?" Sydney asked quietly, looking at the floor.

"It's not important."

"Yes, it is. I want to know."

"Sydney, you're none of those things. Why do you care what people think?"

"I'm trying to fit in here."

"Why do you really want to be like everyone else?" Finn shook his head. "Backstabbing liars and rumor spreaders . . ."

"They're not all like that." Sydney caught his gaze. "I'm not like that." She paused at her words, surprised she had said them. She *was* like that, wasn't she?

Finn nodded. "I agree. That's why we're friends." He got up and took their trays. "Let's go outside and talk. It's nice out."

Sydney followed him outside, and they sat in the grass near the fence.

"What are you doing this weekend?" he asked.

"I'm going to a funeral."

"Oh . . . I'm sorry. Who died?"

"Mary. She's a good friend of my mom's."

"And of yours, too?"

"Yeah."

"I'm sorry. What happened?"

"She died in her sleep."

"That's the way to go."

Sydney's eyes narrowed. "What?"

Finn shrugged. "Well, if you're gonna go, that's the way to do it, isn't it? No pain, just drifting off to sleep."

"I guess."

"So what's an Ojibwa funeral like?"

"Nowadays, it can be a mixture of traditional and Christian."

"What's the traditional part like?"

Sydney thought for a moment before speaking. "Native people believe that we just occupy this physical body during our lifetime. We are put here to be caretakers for the land and to walk our path. When we die, a spiritual leader will guide our spirit to another world."

"How do they do that?"

"Relatives are given a list of items from the spiritual leader. On the list are things like moccasins."

"If the person is dead, why do they need moccasins?" asked Finn, frowning. He picked up a blade of grass and tried to blow into it to make a buzzing sound. It didn't work, and Sydney laughed.

"Because the person who had died will walk down a path that others before them took," said Sydney. "They will recognize the moccasins of others who have gone before them."

"I see. What else?"

"Well, the rituals last five days, and that will include a fire, starting on the first day outside the person's house. Tobacco and food are offered to the spirit. They are put in birchbark baskets to feed the soul as it makes its journey."

"What kind of food?"

"Things like venison, wild rice, and fish."

"They eat on their way to heaven?" asked Finn, grinning.

Sydney laughed. "You could put it that way."

She smiled and looked away, and Finn tilted his head to one side and caught her glance.

"What are you smiling for?" he asked, and she shrugged.

"After their journey, they arrive at *Gaagige Minawaanigoziwining*, which means 'the land of everlasting happiness.' When they see the northern lights, that's our people up there, dancing."

Finn smiled. "That must be a beautiful sight."

Sydney nodded.

"So, when are you leaving for the funeral?"

"Tonight."

"Is the funeral being held on the reservation?"

"Yes."

"I bet you miss your friends. Maybe you can see them while you're there."

"I plan to."

"Good. Hey, how about if I walk you home tonight? I can have my dad pick me up from there."

"You don't have to do that."

"Sure I do. I bet your mom wasn't too happy you let a boy she doesn't know and his father drive you home. Maybe I can meet her."

"How did you know that?"

"Well, I'd be upset if it was my daughter."

Sydney laughed at his expression. "Yeah, she wasn't too thrilled."

"What did you tell her?"

"I told her you guys were cool."

"Oh, well, thanks for that. But I bet she'd like to make up her own mind."

"Yeah, probably."

"So, I will meet you at the front door right after school."

"Alright."

He reached in his pocket and took out his phone.

"Hey, you're not supposed to have that in school," said Sydney, looking around.

"I know." He put the phone up to his ear and paused. "Shoot, he didn't answer. Hi, Dad. Don't pick me up from school this afternoon. I'm walking Sydney home. You can pick me up there. I'll call you later."

He hung up and shoved the phone back in his pocket.

"So, what are *you* going to do this weekend?" asked Sydney.

"I don't know. Homework for sure. I have a ton of math to do. Dad can help me, though. He's an engineer."

"Oh, I didn't know that. What's your dad like?"

"He's left-brained, you know. He likes things neat and orderly."

"What's your mother like?"

Finn didn't answer for a moment, thinking. "Well, she's a homemaker. I mean, she didn't work outside the home when my parents were together. She's kind of old-fashioned. She likes to cook and sew."

"My mom is an office administrator for a large company in St. Paul," said Sydney. "She runs the office and works for the vice president of the company. She seems to like it a lot."

"That's good."

"Sometimes she can work remotely from her home office."

"Are you guys close?"

"Yes."

"And your father?"

"Gone," stated Sydney. "Moved out and away. I don't know exactly where he lives, and I don't care."

"I take it you two don't get along?"

"He was never satisfied with anything involving me," answered Sydney. "I made straight A's at the reservation school, but he always found a way to make me feel like that wasn't good enough. He was always pushing me to do more, do better, be the best." She sighed. "I hated it."

"And him? How do you feel about him?"

"I don't know anymore. He's still pushing Mom and me, but from the outside now. Mom's had enough, and so have I."

"Do you see him?"

"Rarely."

"Is that his choice or yours?"

"Mine."

The warning bell rang, and Sydney and Finn got up to go to class. They waved goodbye at the front door, and as Sydney took a right inside the building, Finn went left.

After school, they arrived at the front door at the same time. They smiled at each other and headed down the steps and down the road.

It wasn't long before Sydney's tormentors started up their usual banter as they walked by, and, as usual, she tried to ignore them.

This time, however, they started harassing Finn, too. Finn tried to ignore them as well, until someone threw a rock that hit him in the face. He dropped to the ground in pain, kneeling on the sidewalk. When Sydney saw the blood running down his face, she'd had enough. The old Sydney took over as she glanced around and then took a step toward them. They kept on laughing, until Sydney dropped her book bag on the ground. One of the boys asked if she was going to scalp them, and she gave them a smile that made more than one of them uncomfortable.

As she stared at each of them, Sydney realized that she had been just like them not so long ago. She would have been the leader of that crowd, laughing and harassing poor Finn as he lay bleeding on the ground. She was uncomfortable for a moment, as she realized the tables were now turned.

What goes around comes around, she thought to herself. Maybe she deserved this treatment for her past mistakes with Autumn, but Finn did not.

Relying on the old Sydney for a moment to make her fearless, she gestured to them to come closer, and when no one moved, she laughed.

"Pretty brave over there, aren't you? But no one here will stand face-to-face with a girl?" She snickered. "Cowards."

Finn watched her with astonishment. A couple of the boys moved forward then, trying to save face. Sydney met them halfway.

"Let me tell you something," she snapped, and then bent over to whisper something to them. She patted the pocket of her coat, and they glanced down at it and then back up into her eyes. Not liking what they saw there, they took a step back. The color left their faces as they quickly turned and walked away, pulling the others with them.

Sydney walked back to Finn, helped him up, and gave him a tissue out of her backpack. With one last look at the now-silent crowd, she and Finn continued their walk home.

"You okay?" she asked.

"I think so," he replied, dabbing at the wound. "It just missed my eye."

She glanced at it and saw that it was still bleeding. "It's a facial wound," she said when she saw his distress over the blood. "They always bleed more."

He nodded, and they were silent as they walked. It wasn't until they cut through Sydney's yard that Finn glanced at her.

"You were pretty scary back there. What did you say to them to get them to back off?"

Sydney smiled. "It's not important. I would be surprised if they bother us ever again, though."

They stopped and sat down on Sydney's front step. Finn pulled out his phone and called his dad to pick him up. Then he shoved the phone back into his pocket and turned to look at her.

"You're very surprising," he said, shaking his head. "That group has been giving you a hard time for weeks. Why did you decide to stand up for yourself now?"

"I didn't."

"What do you mean? I saw you . . ."

"I stood up for *you*. The fact that they will probably leave both of us alone now is a bonus."

"But you must have said something pretty powerful."

Sydney shrugged.

"Come on. What did you say?"

Sydney shrugged again, and Finn laughed.

"Really? You're not going to tell me?"

"Okay, so I told them yesterday I called the police on them and they were being watched at the moment. They were going to arrest all of them, and we were filing charges. They would get expelled from school." Sydney pushed her hair out of her face and added, "And this was their last chance to leave us alone before they spent the holidays in juvie."

"Juvie?"

"Yeah, you know. Juvenile detention."

"And they bought that?"

Sydney shrugged. "Apparently. They backed off."

"You didn't really call the police, did you?"

"Nope."

"Then how come they believed you?"

"I noticed a police car pull up down the road from us. The officer was still in the car when I told them that." Sydney grinned. "He was very convincing. I was grateful he was there."

"Boy, you can sure think fast on your feet." Finn dabbed at his wound and then asked, "What's in your pocket?"

"My pocket?"

"Yeah. I saw you patting your pocket when you were talking to those guys. What's in there?"

Sydney slowly reached into her pocket and pulled out a small brush. Finn frowned.

"It's a brush."

"Yup."

"So . . . I don't get it. They seemed scared . . ."

Sydney smiled. "They didn't know it was a brush."

Finn stared at her wide-eyed. "Did they think it was a gun?"

Sydney laughed and shook her head. "No. They probably thought it was a knife."

"What? You told them you had a knife in your pocket?"

She shook her head. "No. I just made a comment about how Native people deal with their enemies."

Finn laughed and shook his head. "The look in their eyes was priceless. You amaze me, Sydney."

She grinned back, and they were quiet for a moment. Then Finn turned to glance at her.

"Why did you stand up for me when you wouldn't stand up for yourself?"

She looked away. "You know, for some reason, it was easier. I deserve to be treated that way. You do not."

"I don't understand."

She was quiet for a moment and then turned to face him.

"I was them, back at the rez school. I was their leader."

"What?"

Sydney shook her head and tried to find the right words.

"I teased and tormented this girl at school, Autumn. I don't know why I did it. She never did anything to me. But I wouldn't leave her alone. It made me feel . . . I don't know . . . better than her in some way."

"What happened?"

"I moved."

"So you tormented her and then moved?"

"Yup."

"You haven't spoken to her since?"

"Nope."

"So she still thinks you hate her?"

"Well, our last couple of conversations were different. But I didn't apologize."

"Why?"

Sydney looked down at the ground. "I was ashamed of my behavior."

"Isn't that all the more reason to apologize?"

"Probably."

Finn shook his head. "So, underneath it all, you still have that in you?"

Sydney shrugged. "Don't we all?"

"Yeah, but not all of us act on it."

Sydney looked away and said nothing, as Finn tended to his wound, which had finally stopped bleeding. His father came shortly afterward and Sydney explained what happened. He thanked her, and he and Finn left.

Sydney sat back down on the step and closed her eyes. She could still hear Finn's words echoing in her mind: "So, underneath it all, you still have that in you?"

She was still sitting there two hours later, when her mom came home.

The Apology

Mary's funeral was well attended. There was some murmuring in the crowd when they realized Mary had been cremated, as it wasn't the Ojibwa way. But her daughter, Marah, sang a beautiful song in Ojibwa, and that seemed to help appease some of the elders.

It wasn't until Sydney was sitting in a fast-food place across from Jayden and Bre that she started thinking about Finn again.

"So, have you replaced us yet?" asked Bre, munching on a french fry.

"I bet you have a lot of friends by now," said Jayden.

"I have a friend named Finn," replied Sydney, opening the wrapper of her hamburger.

"What's he like?" asked Jayden.

Sydney shrugged. "He's nice."

"That's it? He's nice?" Bre laughed. "Sounds like a real gem."

"Wait, you only have *one* friend?" Jayden laughed. "You're kidding, right?"

"What about you guys?" asked Sydney, trying to change the subject. "What have you been up to since I've been gone?"

"Well, Autumn and Adam are going at it hot and heavy," replied Bre. "He took her to the dance last week and . . ."

"I don't care about Autumn. I'm asking about you guys."

Bre and Jayden stopped eating to look at Sydney.

"That's what I was talking about," replied Bre. "We're still on Autumn's case. She's like high and mighty over having a boyfriend, and we aren't having any of that."

"Meaning?"

"Meaning, we like to knock her down a peg or two," answered Jayden, licking the salt off her fingers from the french fries.

"So that's all you've been doing since I left?" Sydney shook her head. "Sounds boring."

Jayden and Bre stared at her and then Bre shook her head.

"It's the same as it's always been. The only change is that you're not there anymore." She shrugged. "School's boring. You know that."

Sydney let the conversation go on, with her friends talking about their vacations and new clothes. Sydney ate in silence, nodding here and there so her friends would think she was interested.

They left her on the curb, waiting for her mother to pick her up. They had offered to drive her back to the hotel, but Sydney had turned them down. She had hugged them both and promised to stay in touch, and then she had watched them leave.

"Sydney?"

Sydney looked over and saw Autumn and Adam approaching the front door of the fast-food place. She nodded.

"I didn't know you were back," said Autumn.

"I came back for Mary's funeral."

"Mary Red Feather? Oh yeah, I heard she had started her soul journey," said Adam. "How long are you here for?"

"I go back tomorrow."

"I see." Adam reached out a hand and Autumn slipped hers into it. "I'm hungry. Let's go eat."

"Autumn, can I talk to you for a moment?" asked Sydney, and Adam's eyes narrowed.

"I'm not so sure . . ." he began to say but was interrupted by Autumn.

"It's okay," she said. He hesitated and then dropped her hand.

"Alright. I'll go order our food and find a table."

"Okay."

A moment later, he was gone, and Sydney led Autumn to the picnic table on the side of the building.

They sat down, and for a moment, no one spoke. Then Sydney turned to look at Autumn.

"I have a friend like you back in Minneapolis," she said.

"Oh? I'm not sure what that means."

"He's gay."

"You think I'm gay?" Autumn laughed. "I can assure you . . ."

"No, I didn't mean it that way."

"Well, what way did you mean it, then?"

"I mean, people at school give him a hard time because of it."

"They pick on him?"

"I guess you could call it that."

"Like you picked on me?"

"Worse."

"That's awful."

"I know."

"You do?"

Sydney shrugged and looked away. "I do now."

Autumn frowned, not understanding where the conversation was going.

"So, you're telling me this because . . .?"

"I'm sorry."

"Sorry?"

Sydney took a deep breath and the words came tumbling out.

"I'm sorry I didn't leave you alone. I'm sorry I made you feel bad. I'm sorry Jayden and Bre are still tormenting you. I'm sorry . . ."

"Wait. What?"

"I'm apologizing here," replied Sydney, defensively.

"Why?"

"Because I thought it was just a little harmless fun, until I became the brunt of everyone's jokes."

"Oh, I see." Autumn smiled. "You're being harassed now, aren't you? What don't they like that you can't change? Your skin color? Your eyes? How tall you are? How short?"

The truth of Autumn's words echoed in her mind: "What don't they like that you can't change?"

"I'm Native."

Autumn nodded. "You moved to Minneapolis? I suspect you're one of the only ones in the whole school."

"There are others. But they don't seem to have the same issues I do."

"Why do you stand out?"

"I've been trying to figure that out myself."

Autumn paused a moment and then turned to look at Sydney.

"How does it feel to have the tables turned?"

Sydney shook her head and didn't answer, and for a moment, Autumn felt sorry for her.

She glanced in through the large fast-food restaurant window and saw Adam gesturing for her to come inside.

"Look, I have to go now," said Autumn, rising from the bench. "Thanks for the apology. I do appreciate it. But I have moved on. Jayden and Bre don't bother me in the least anymore." She smiled. "I know they think they do, but I just don't care." She glanced through the window again and smiled. "I'm happy with my life now, so don't worry about it. It's all good."

She stepped away, adding, "Have a safe trip back."

Sydney's mother pulled up a few minutes later and she got into the car. Sydney glanced over at her and realized her mother had changed out of her funeral clothes and into a pair of jeans and a Twins baseball jersey. A baseball cap was sitting backwards on her head, and she looked about sixteen years old.

Sydney sighed, feeling like the old one in the car, and leaned her head against the car door. She thought apologizing to Autumn would make her feel better, but it didn't. And she hadn't heard from Finn since their encounter with the bullies. She now wondered if he was upset with her for telling him about her past.

Dakotah glanced at her daughter. She thought Jayden and Bre would have cheered her up, but apparently not.

"You okay over there?"

Sydney turned to look at her mother. "Yeah, just thinking. I saw Autumn a few minutes ago. She was here with Adam."

"I see. How did that go?"

"Okay."

"Just okay?"

"I apologized to her for having given her such a hard time."

"That's good. What did she say?"

"She thanked me and said she had moved on with her life and is happy now."

"Well, that's good to hear, right?"

"I guess."

"So, what's the matter then?"

"I don't know. I guess I'm not happy with myself for doing that to her."

"Sounds like you should forgive yourself."

"I don't know how."

Her mother glanced over at her. "It's something you'll have to figure out, that's all."

"Sounds like a lot of work."

Dakotah laughed. "You aren't one for extra work, are you. Everything comes easy to you, doesn't it. School did, anyway. Your dad was always pushing you to do better because you always got the work done ahead of time and never put in any more effort to go the extra distance."

"He was never satisfied . . ."

"Nor should *you* be," said her mother. "You should want to be all you can be. What kind of life is it to laze around and not go the extra mile?"

"I don't laze around."

"You do your homework but never take on extra projects."

"So? My grades are good enough."

"I see."

"What?"

Dakotah smiled and replied, "So you just want to be 'good enough.'"

"Everyone wants to be good enough," answered Sydney, defensively now.

"You're twisting my words in a way I don't mean them," replied her mother. She laughed. "You should become a lawyer."

Sydney shrugged. "I don't know what I want to be yet. I have time to decide."

"I guess so. The term 'go-getter' is not in your vocabulary, is it."

"Mother, I am not in the mood for this conversation."

"I'm just saying you have to go the extra mile to figure out what kind of person you want to be and then work on becoming that. It's okay to have regrets, but not if they hold you back from continuing on with your life."

"That's a lot of flowery phrasing, Mom. What are you trying to say?"

"Let it go and move on."

"Why didn't you just say that in the first place?"

"I like the flowery phrases."

Dakotah laughed, and Sydney gave her a reluctant smile as she took in what her mother was saying. She leaned back in the seat and smiled. Her mother was probably right, but she would never tell her that.

Forgive Yourself

Did you see your mother?" asked Sydney as she sat down across from Finn. He looked up from his salad and shook his head.

"I took a note from your book and told Dad no."

"Really?"

"Yup. Mom wasn't too happy." Finn smiled and Sydney frowned back.

"I bet," she said. "So did you really not want to see her or were you getting her back for a wrong you think she committed against you?"

"Wow, those are some big phrases."

"Yeah, my mom thinks I should become a lawyer. But you didn't answer my question."

He shrugged. "A little of both, I guess."

"So now what?"

"Now, I'm going to finish my lunch and go outside and sit."

"That's not what I meant . . ."

"I don't want to talk about it . . ."

"But . . ."

"Sydney . . ."

"Alright, never mind."

Sydney took a drink of her milk and picked up her fork to start eating.

"Your face looks okay now," she observed, and he nodded.

"Yeah, Dad put some stuff on it."

"You walking home tonight after school?"

"Dad won't let me."

Sydney nodded. "I can understand that."

"To be honest, I'm getting tired of dealing with those people," he said, dropping his fork with a clatter onto his tray.

"Those people?"

"You know, the ones who think they're smarter and better than you so they push you around like you're nothing. I'm just sick of it."

"I'm sure you are," replied Sydney, looking down at her tray now. Finn's words stung, as the truth of what he said hit home. Wasn't she one of "those people"?

"I mean, they have been doing this since last year," Finn went on. He shook his head. "I guess some people never grow up."

"I guess."

"You would think they would find something better to do with their time."

"Yeah." Sydney set her fork down as Finn went on.

"I hate them. All of them."

"I'm sorry." There was a pause, and then Sydney asked a question that had been on her mind for a while now.

"Do you think they can change and become better people?" she asked, staring into his eyes.

"I have yet to see it happen."

"I see." Sydney looked down at her tray again as his words sunk in. Her eyes started to tear up, and she wanted to get up and leave. She had been hit with what she thought could possibly be the most important truth of her life: Once a bully, always a bully. Could she actually change that part about herself, the part that wanted to lash out and hurt people to make herself feel better? "Get them before they get you," her father always said.

"Sydney?"

She looked up and saw Finn gazing at her with concern. She blinked the tears away and smiled.

"I'm okay." She picked up her fork and started eating again. "Good salad, huh? My mom puts olives and deli meat in her chef's salad . . ."

"Sydney."

"I like ranch dressing, but Mom always buys vinaigrette . . ."

"Sydney!" Finn reached out to take the fork from her hand. "What's wrong?" he asked.

She shook her head and stood up with her tray. "I have to go," she muttered. "I just remembered I need to grab my homework out of my locker before my next class."

Finn was off the bench and around the table before she could move. He took the tray out of her hands and dropped it on the table.

"Come on," he said, and with a hand on her back he started guiding her out the cafeteria door.

"But my tray," protested Sydney, but Finn just shook his head.

"They'll get it," he replied, opening the door and walking with her around the building.

They headed for the other side of the grassy lawn and sat down on it.

"Okay, out with it," he said, staring at her. "What did I say wrong?"

"Nothing."

He shook his head.

"Then what's up? You were almost in tears back there." He sighed and leaned forward. "I can't lose my best friend over something stupid I said. Now out with it."

"Your best friend?"

"Well," he replied, smiling, "you are my only friend, so that makes you my best one, right?"

Sydney laughed, and Finn relaxed a little and sat back.

"Talk."

Sydney shook her head, and he leaned forward again, thinking.

Finn went over their conversation in his head. A moment of clarity came to him and he frowned, glancing at her.

"Oh, I get it now," he said, shaking his head.

"You do?"

"I wasn't talking about you, Sydney."

She said nothing, and he sighed.

"I'm sorry I got so upset over those good-for-nothings that won't leave me alone," he said. "But you're nothing like them."

"I was."

"But now you're not." He moved closer to her in the grass. "Look, I admit, I was surprised when you told me you used to bully someone. But you're not like that anymore."

"I bullied those idiots who were following us home."

Finn shook his head. "No, you stood up for me . . . for us. That's a positive use of your skills."

"My skills?"

"Yeah. I think being assertive is a skill."

Sydney shook her head. "I don't think Autumn thought I was just being assertive when I harassed her."

"The girl on the reservation you bothered?"

"'Bothered' is putting it mildly," she replied, looking away.

"Okay, so you bullied and harassed a girl for no good reason. You frustrated her, made her mad, and made her feel less than she was, and generally beat her down?"

"Yes."

"Do you know why?"

"No. Yes." She sighed. "Maybe."

"Are you planning to continue the behavior?"

"No."

"Is that because she's not here and there's no one around worth beating up with your words?"

Sydney snickered and glanced at the group of students gathered by the picnic tables. They were giving her and Finn looks and whispering and laughing.

"No."

"Then why stop?"

"I don't want to do it anymore."

"Why?"

Sydney pulled her knees up to her chest and sighed. "I don't like that person."

"So what's the problem?"

Sydney shook her head. "I was hateful back then. I did some terrible things."

"But you're not that person anymore. You have to forgive yourself and move on."

"That's what my mother said, too. But I don't know how."

Finn took her hand and made her look into his eyes. "Just close your eyes and whisper, 'I forgive myself for who I used to be.' Let those words go into your soul and heal you."

"Wow," she said. "That's deep."

He grinned. "Thanks. I hit the mark sometimes."

"You know, my grandmother once told me if you whisper to the sky, it will take the words where you want them to go."

"Now that's deep," replied Finn, and she smiled.

"I had forgotten all about the conversations we used to have." Sydney paused and looked away. "She's gone now."

"Is she?"

Sydney looked over at Finn with new respect in her eyes. "You're a smart guy."

"I know."

Sydney smiled, and he sighed. "Now, if I could just get my best friend to let me take her home tonight, life would be perfect."

"Why is that such a big deal?"

"It's my birthday today. Consider it my present."

"It's your birthday? Why didn't you tell me? We could have celebrated. I would have given you a gift."

Finn shrugged. "I stopped having birthday celebrations the year I came out to my parents."

"That's terrible."

"Yeah, I guess the day I was born isn't much of a celebration for them. At least not for my mother anyway."

"Oh, Finn." Sydney reached out and hugged him. He stiffened a moment and then hugged her back.

"You know," he whispered, "that's the first hug I've had in a long time."

Sydney hugged him harder until he pushed her away, laughing.

"Hey, that's enough now," he said. "Otherwise, people are going to think I'm straight."

Sydney laughed and took his hand. "Thanks for everything, Finn. I'm so lucky to have a friend like you."

Finn smiled back. "I've waited a long time to hear those words."

They got up holding hands and walked back into the building. Separating at the door, they each went to class and finished out the day. Sydney met him by the front door after school with a homemade birthday card in her hand. She offered it to him with a grin, and his eyes got mysteriously damp as he took it.

He opened it slowly and read the poem she had written for him. Then he unfolded the slip of paper she had added and gave her a watery smile.

"A free supper, huh? That could be a good or bad present depending on how well you cook."

"Hey, I'm a good cook."

"So you say. I will be the judge of that," he replied, grinning. "So, what are we eating? Some corn hotdish or corn salad or corn . . ."

"Excuse me! Natives eat more than corn."

"Really? I thought their whole diet was based on corn products," he said, chuckling as she slugged him playfully.

"I'm not going to tell my mother you said that," she said, smiling back. "I want her to like you."

"What's not to like?" he asked solemnly, and she shook her head as they walked over to his dad's car that had just arrived.

Sydney opened the door and gestured for Finn to get in. He smiled and then slid into the car, pulling a laughing Sydney in with him. His father grinned as he drove away.

Finding Her Voice

Sydney stood with her mother, nervously glancing up and down the hall. Dakotah was talking to her lawyer, who had been recommended by someone she worked with.

Sydney didn't want to be in the hall. She was so afraid her father would spot her and try to make a scene. She nervously pushed her hair back behind her ear and straightened her clothes for the third time.

"Stop fidgeting," said Dakotah, nodding to the lawyer as he walked away. "Come on, let's go inside and wait."

Glad to be out of the hall, Sydney stuck to her mother like glue as they entered the courtroom. It was almost empty except for her father, who sat in the front row. She caught her breath, hoping he wouldn't turn around and notice them there.

Her father was shuffling through some paperwork as Sydney and her mother sat in the back row in the corner. One by one, people shuffled in, filling the seats.

"Just relax, Sydney," instructed her mother.

"I'm trying, but Dad is right there . . ."

"I know where he is." Dakotah sighed. "Sorry about that. He makes me nervous, too."

The bailiff stood and announced the entrance of the judge, and everyone stood up. It was then that Sydney's father looked around and noticed them in the back row. Sydney kept her eyes on the judge as her father tried to catch her attention.

"Be seated, please," instructed the bailiff, and Sydney and Dakotah sat down. Sydney noticed that her mother was ignoring her father, too, and she reached out to take her hand. It was cold and clammy, and Sydney knew then she was scared to death.

Several cases were ahead of theirs, and people came in and out of the courtroom. Then, before she knew it, their case was called.

"Dakotah Coffman, please step forward."

Her mother rose, and with as much courage as she could muster, stepped forward to stand in front of the judge.

The judge asked her some questions and glanced at Sydney now and then. Dakotah responded calmly, asking the judge for supervised visitation for Sydney. The judge was reluctant to do so and told her mother as much. Their lawyer then submitted signed documents from the school Sydney attended describing her father's disastrous visit there. Dakotah then went on to talk about the verbal abuse she and Sydney had endured while living with him.

"Sydney and her mother both agree that he should be able to see her," said their lawyer in closing, "but since he has a past of not being able to control himself verbally, as well as what happened at the school, we think it is in Sydney's best interests that he be supervised during that time."

The judge looked at Sydney a moment, thinking over the situation.

Dakotah sighed and took a step forward. "Your honor, my daughter has been through a lot. She would like her father to get help because she still sees something good in him. But she's afraid of him now, and I hope you understand my reluctance in having his visitation be unsupervised. He has a bad temper. I would hate for something to happen."

Her father's lawyer interjected then. "Your honor, Roger has never hurt his child physically. According to him, his words have always been well intended and said to further push the child to do better academically."

The judge looked over at Sydney and gestured for her to see him. He put the court in a short recess and took Sydney down the hall into his office.

"Have a seat, Sydney."

Sydney did as she was told, and the judge sat down at his desk, leaning back a little. He smiled at her, noting her nervousness.

"I just wanted to talk with you for a few minutes," he said, cleaning his glasses before shoving them back on again. "How do you see this situation between your parents?"

"Sir?"

"What do you want out of all this?"

Sydney sat quietly for a moment, organizing her thoughts.

"I want my dad to go to counseling," she said. "I think he has some issues left over from his childhood that he's dragging into the present." She looked down at her feet and added, "He doesn't treat me very well."

"Has he ever hurt you?"

"Yes, but not physically." Sydney looked up at him and added, "I think I'm just a bother to him, just another thing he has to deal with."

"Why do you think that?"

Sydney shook her head. "He never hugs me. He never tells me he loves me." Sydney sat back in her chair with a sigh. "He probably wishes I hadn't been born."

"Those are tough words."

"It was tough saying them."

The judge nodded. "I read all the case notes. Everyone you have spoken to about this has spoken highly of you. You have a great future ahead of you."

"Thank you." Sydney glanced up at the judge and shrugged. "I'm afraid of him. He's unpredictable." She paused and looked away. "He doesn't want me," she added softly. "I don't understand why he's trying to see me all the time."

The judge stared at her. This young girl touched something inside of him that he had carried around with him since childhood. There had been no one to help him back then, but he would do what he could to help her now.

"Thank you for being honest with me," he said, standing. She stood as well and glanced over at him.

"So, what's going to happen now?" she asked.

"We're going back into the courtroom, where I am going to grant the supervised visitation. There's no way I'm going to let the light inside of you go out."

Sydney was surprised at his words and watched him as he went silent for a moment.

"I understand the situation," he said. "I, too, went through something similar growing up. Things happened differently for me. My light was snuffed out, and it took me a long time before I could get it lit again." He smiled over at her. "I want something better for you."

They entered the courtroom, where her parents sat waiting. The judge asked Roger to approach the bench, which he did. The judge bent over and spoke quietly to Roger for a moment and then sat back. Roger looked at the floor and then slowly backed away.

The judge gave his decision to order supervised visitation. The matter would be revisited in six months. Sydney, her parents, and their lawyers left the courtroom.

As Dakotah signed paperwork, Sydney stood quietly beside her. She felt sorry for her father but was relieved she wouldn't have to deal with him on her own for a while.

"Sydney."

Sydney looked behind her to see her father standing there with his lawyer. He tried to go toward her, but his lawyer put out a hand and shook his head.

He shook off his lawyer's hand. "I want to see you."

"You're seeing me now," she replied quietly.

He snickered. "You know what I mean." His gaze went to Dakotah, who had finished signing the paperwork.

"And you. You did this. You poisoned her against me."

Before Dakotah could stop her, Sydney strode up to her father.

"You did this to yourself," she said, pointing at him.

"Don't you talk to me like that," he said, his eyes narrowing. "I'm your father."

"It's just a word," she whispered. "And I suggest you look it up. Because it doesn't mean what you think it does."

"Excuse me?"

"One of us grew up, Dad." Sydney turned to go, adding, "And it wasn't you."

"What's gotten into you?" he asked angrily, reaching out to grab her arm.

She shrugged it off and looked him square in the face. "I guess I just found my voice." She sighed. "Maybe you really do think you were doing the right thing in how you dealt with me, but you were wrong. Just because your father treated you that way does not make it right. You should know that. Get some help so you can be the father I deserve, or get out of my life so I can move on."

The lawyer had to restrain her father as Dakotah took Sydney's arm and headed down the hallway to the elevator. It wasn't until they reached the car and got in that either of them spoke.

"You have a great capacity for language," her mother said as she started the car. "I really do think you should become a lawyer."

"Maybe."

"You dealt with your father in a very adult fashion. I'm proud of you."

"Thanks."

"If he gets counseling, then hopefully things will get better between you two."

"Maybe."

"Can you ever forgive him for the way he's treated you over the years?"

Sydney glanced at her. "Yes, I think so."

"Then why can't you forgive yourself?"

Sydney, surprised at the question, sighed. For a few moments, they both were quiet, as her mother moved the car out of the parking lot and into traffic.

"You must have said something special to the judge, Sydney. I didn't think he was going to grant me that order."

Sydney shrugged. "I just told him the truth."

Dakotah nodded, and they headed home in silence.

After supper that night, Sydney went outside to sit on the step. It was almost dark, but the night air smelled crisp and warm around her.

Closing her eyes, she sighed, glad this day was over. She had finally faced her dad without fear. She just hoped her father heard her and would begin to work on himself. She really did want him in her life. Despite it all, she loved him. He had some good qualities, and she caught glimpses of them from time to time.

Opening her eyes again, she gazed up at the stars she was starting to see in the sky. She liked to pick out the big dipper and noticed the little dipper close by. It was like they were friends, and she thought about Finn then, grateful he had chosen her to be his.

He was smart and wise, and his words floated through her head, taking shape. She closed her eyes again and thanked the Gitchie Manitou for bringing him into her life.

"Please help me to be a better person," she whispered to the sky. "I'm so sorry for everything I did to Autumn. Please help me forgive myself."

An owl hooted, which made her jump. Laughing a bit, she settled down on the step again and thought back to something her grandmother had told her when she was little.

"Seeing or hearing an owl means death," she had said, "but it doesn't have to be the death of a person. It can be the death of a way of life, or a transition. It's also believed owls carry messages back and forth from the heavens to Earth."

Sydney sighed. She glanced at the sky again and smiled.

Hopefully, her grandmother was right.

RESOURCES

PACER'S NATIONAL BULLYING PREVENTION CENTER

pacer.org/bullying

PACER's National Bullying Prevention Center actively leads social change to prevent childhood bullying so that all youth are safe and supported in their schools, communities, and online. PACER provides innovative resources for students, parents, educators, and others, and recognizes bullying as a serious community issue that negatively affects education, physical and emotional health, and the safety and well-being of students.

COMMITTEE FOR CHILDREN

cfchildren.org/programs/bullying-prevention

Committee for Children helps empower kids and the adults around them by supplying information and resources to understand what bullying is, who is affected by it, and what the community can do to prevent it.

NATIONAL ASSOCIATION OF ELEMENTARY SCHOOL PRINCIPALS

naesp.org/bullying-prevention-resources

Maintaining a safe, nurturing school environment for students is any school leader's top priority. The resources provided by NAESP can help principals and teachers combat bullying in their schools.

StopBullying.gov

StopBullying.gov provides information from various government agencies on what bullying is, what cyberbullying is, who is at risk, and the best ways to prevent and respond to bullying.

AMERICAN ACADEMY OF CHILD & ADOLESCENT PSYCHIATRY

Bullying Resource Center

aacap.org/AACAP/Families_and_Youth/Resource_ Centers/Bullying_Resource_Center/Home.aspx

Child and adolescent psychiatrists are trained to look out for signs that a child is the victim of bullying. They can help concerned parents take the proper plan of action to make sure their children get all the support they need to stay resilient and confident.

THE LGBT NATIONAL HOTLINE
glbthotline.org/hotline.html

The LGBT hotline provides a safe, anonymous, and confidential space where callers can speak on many different issues and concerns, including coming out, gender and/or sexuality identity, bullying, and much more.

STOMP OUT BULLYING
stompoutbullying.org/helpchat

The goal of the STOMP Out Bullying live HelpChat Line is to help reduce the stress, depression, and fear that can result from being bullied and to empower those who have been bullied to make healthy decisions.

ABOUT THE AUTHOR

KIM SIGAFUS is an award-winning Ojibwa writer and Illinois Humanities Road Scholars speaker. She has coauthored two 7th Generation books in the Native Trailblazers series of biographies, including *Native Elders: Sharing Their Wisdom* and the award-winning *Native Writers: Voices of Power*. Her fiction work includes the PathFinders novels *Nowhere to Hide*, *Autumn's Dawn*, and *Finding Grace*, which are the first three books in the Autumn Dawn series. She is also the author of The Mida, an eight-volume series about a mystically powerful time-traveling carnival owned by an Ojibwa woman. Kim's family is from the White Earth Reservation in northern Minnesota. She resides with her husband in Freeport, Illinois. For more information, visit kimberlysigafus.com.

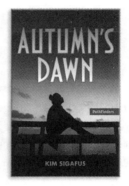